MEET THE GIRL TAL

Sabrina Wells is petite, with curly auburn hair, sparkling hazel eyes, and a bubbly personality. Sabrina loves magazines, shopping, sleepovers, and most of all, she loves talking to her best friends.

Katie Campbell is a straight-A student and super athlete. With her blond hair, blue eyes, and matching clothes, she's everyone's idea of little miss perfect. But Katie has a few surprises for everyone, including herself!

Randy Zak has just moved to Acorn Falls from New York City, and is she ever cool! With her radical spiked haircut and her hip New York clothes, Randy teaches everyone just how much fun it is to be different.

Allison Cloud is a Native American Indian. Allison's super smart and really beautiful. But she has one major problem: She's thirteen years old, five foot seven, and still growing!

Here's what they're talking about in

Girl Talk

KATIE:	Hi, Sabs. I knew it was you the minute I heard the phone ring.
SABRINA:	I've just been dying to talk to you since lunch.
KATIE:	I've been dying to talk to you, too!
SABRINA:	About what? You've really got me worried. And I'm worried enough as it is.
KATIE:	You are?
SABRINA:	Sure. And I think it's about the same thing you're worried about.
KATIE:	You mean about Stacy's disappearing act?
SABRINA:	So, you noticed it, too?

THE WINNING TEAM

By L. E. Blair

GIRL TALK® series created by Western Publishing Company, Inc.

Produced by Angel Entertainment, Inc.

Western Publishing Company, Inc., Racine, Wisconsin 53404

 Library of Congress Catalog Card Number 91-70583
ISBN: 0-307-22013-3/ MCMXCI

Text by Carol McCarren

Chapter One

"Wake up, Sabs," I heard Allison Cloud, one of my best friends, whisper suddenly as she nudged her elbow against mine.

"What? Who's there?" I blurted out, lifting my head quickly from my desk and sending my math textbook crashing to the floor.

"Sabrina Wells!" Miss Munson, our math teacher, who is also known as the Dragon Lady, bellowed. "I certainly hope we're not keeping you awake this morning . . ."

With a start, I remembered where I was. Tuesday morning. First-period math class. Actually, I hadn't really been sleeping. I'd been thinking about the school elections that were coming up in a few weeks. But I had a feeling that it wouldn't be a great idea to admit that to Miss Munson.

"Umm, no, Miss Munson," I answered, bending down to pick up my book. "Ahh, I was just concentrating . . . hard . . . um . . . on that last . . . um . . . division problem you gave us."

I could feel the whole class staring at me, so I kept my eyes glued to the floor. I hate that feeling — you know the feeling that everyone's looking at you, and you're trying to act like it's no big deal.

"That would require a lot of concentration, Miss Wells," Miss Munson said, "since we're not doing division today."

Without even looking at her, I could tell she was pinching up her face and puckering up her lips. She always does that when she's annoyed. All I could think about was how it makes her look like this vampire rat in one of the gross horror movies one of my other best friends, Randy Zak, loves so much.

"We're working on finding square roots today," Miss Munson went on to inform me.

"Oh! Well, that's probably why I was having so much trouble," I remarked, trying to sound as casual as I could.

The whole class cracked up at that. And I, of course, started doing what I call my body blush. My entire body turns red, all the way up to the top of my head. I'm only four feet eleven and three-quarter inches tall, so it doesn't take very long for me to start looking like a blotchy red pepper. It's pretty embarrassing.

"I'll see you after class for that remark, young lady," Miss Munson said through gritted teeth.

I guess I deserved it for not paying attention. But I hadn't been able to think about anything but the elections since Mr. Hansen, our principal, announced them yesterday. Not that I'm really into politics or anything like that. But it was exciting to think about who might run.

When the bell rang, I glumly marched up to Miss Munson's desk. She began talking right away. I tried very hard but I couldn't concentrate on what she was saying. Thankfully, the warning bell for the next period rang and I heard Miss Munson say that I had better "ship up or shape out" or "shape up or ship out," I wasn't sure. Anyway, I mumbled a promise to do better and ran out of the room.

Luckily, Allison was waiting for me right outside the classroom. As soon as I saw her I rolled my eyes and sighed in relief. Then we both burst out laughing.

"Honestly, Sabrina, you almost did it this time."

"I know, Al! Thanks for helping me out," I said, clasping my hands together. Then we both burst out laughing again.

Al's a lot taller than I am and today, as usual, she looked beautiful. She was wearing a chocolate brown sweater that really brought out the brown in her eyes, along with off-white corduroy pants. Her long black hair hung down her back in its usual braid. Al's a Native American. She's one hundred percent Chippewa. I think that's pretty cool.

I eyed my own outfit skeptically. It had seemed like such a great idea when I was at home in my room, but now I wasn't so sure. I was trying to copy something I saw in *Young Chic*, my absolute favorite magazine. One of the models had on jeans shorts rolled up to just above the knee, over tights. I didn't have any jeans shorts, so I was wearing these big blue gym shorts I borrowed from my older brother, Luke. He's sixteen and six feet tall, so the shorts were about the right length on me but they fit kind of loose and baggy. I was wearing them over a pair of bright yellow tights. It was too late to do anything about my clothes now, though.

I told Al I'd catch up with her in third period homeroom, and dashed off to my locker to get my clarinet for band class. Katie, my best, best friend, who also happens to be my locker partner, was there already, getting out her flute.

"Sabs, you look so . . . uh . . . so . . ." Katie let her voice trail off, and I could tell she was trying to decide what she thought of my outfit.

She was wearing a gray pleated skirt and a gray turtleneck with a blue cardigan sweater over it. The blue headband holding her long, straight blond hair off her face matched her sweater exactly and made her eyes look bluer than ever. Katie's always totally coordinated every day. Not that *I'm* a slob or anything, but I do like to try new things.

"I look so what?" I asked, peering at my reflection in the mirror I had taped up inside our locker door. In addition to the blue shorts and yellow tights, I also had on a green shirt, red flats, and a purple cardigan. My curly auburn hair was like a pouffy reddish-brown crown over everything. I loved all the bright colors together. They kind of made me feel like a human rainbow.

"Different," Katie finally decided.

"Well, shorts and tights instead of skirts are the latest thing," I informed her. "This month's issue of *Young Chic* is full of girls in shorts."

I grabbed my clarinet, closed our locker door, and we hurried to band, sitting down just as the bell rang. Mr. Metcalf, the band instructor, is one of my favorite teachers, but all during class I couldn't seem to keep my mind from wandering. I guess I was tired.

I'd stayed up kind of late reading this great book on acting. See, I plan to be an actress one day. I don't really get a lot of opportunities to act in a small town like Acorn Falls, Minnesota, so I've come up with my own "study at home" program.

Mostly, I watch a lot of old movies and imitate the actresses. But once in a while I take out books from the library on different acting styles. I don't really understand a lot of what they're saying. But I figure that by the time I get into acting school, I'll know the basics.

As we started the next song Mr. Metcalf gave me a funny look when I played a wrong note. After that I forced myself to really concentrate. Somehow I got through the rest of class without making any more mistakes.

When Katie and I got to homeroom, which is also our English class, Randy and Al were already there. They were standing next to Randy's desk.

"Hey, Sabs, you look cool!" Randy complimented me.

Randy is from New York City and she dresses wilder than anyone else at Bradley Junior High, or in all of Acorn Falls for that matter. Today she had on this silver-green tunic with silver buttons up the front over black leggings and her black granny boots. She also has this great spiky black hair, which makes all of her clothes look even cooler.

"Thanks, Ran," I replied with a smile. "Multicolors are the theme this season."

"But, I could use a pair of sunglasses to cut down on the glare," Randy added. She pretended to shade her eyes as she hung the black leather jacket she wears everywhere over the back of her chair.

"I think you look really nice," said Al, smiling softly.

Randy and Allison complement each other

so perfectly. I mean, Al is kind of shy and quiet, while Randy's much more outspoken and outrageous. They really bring out the best in each other. It's kind of like with Katie and me, the way she's so organized while I'm always running in six different directions at once. I guess that's why we're all such good friends. Like my dad always says, "'Variety is the spice of life.'"

"You do kind of look like you might glow in the dark, Sabs," Katie chimed in.

"Maybe you're starting a new trend," Randy commented with a grin. "Glow-in-the-dark wear."

I giggled, imagining everyone at Bradley walking around looking like a bunch of neon signs. "Hey, can I help it if I'm a trendsetter?"

At that moment, the loudspeaker crackled to life. That meant it was time for morning announcements, so Allison and Katie hurried to their seats on the other side of the room. Our loudspeaker must be a hundred years old. Every time someone talks over it, it sounds like they're eating crunchy cereal. Sometimes I just tune it out. But today I listened closely since I knew Mr. Hansen would be talking about the upcoming school elections.

". . . so don't forget, Bradley Junior High is your school, and it's up to you to go out and vote for your officials. Class president, vice president, secretary, and treasurer . . . who will they be this year? The choice is yours," he chatted on through the loudspeaker's static.

I felt a slight thrill well up inside me when Mr. Hansen spoke. These elections are an opportunity for us to make Bradley everything we want it to be. I think that's pretty exciting.

I must have been daydreaming again, because before I knew it the bell was ringing. Randy, Katie, Al, and I dumped our books in our lockers and headed to the cafeteria for lunch. The cafeteria is always totally crowded and loud, but we managed to find a table near the back of the room.

"So, who do you think is going to run for president?" I asked, taking a sip of my cranberry-orange seltzer. I drink seltzer every day, and I like to rotate flavors. Cranberry-orange isn't one of my favorites, but I'm hoping I'll grow to like it more. I think it's important to try lots of different things.

"Like we have a choice about who it's going to be," Randy remarked sarcastically. She popped a radish into her mouth. Randy eats radishes like they're peanuts. Just looking at them gives me shivers. I hate radishes.

"Why do you say that?" Allison asked, unwrapping a piece of homemade corn bread. Allison's grandmother lives with her family, and she always makes Al these incredible lunches. I make my own lunch and put together whatever I feel like eating. Sometimes my combinations don't turn out as great as I think they're going to be.

"What she means is that everyone knows who's going to be the president of the seventh-grade class," Katie explained, bringing me back to the conversation about elections.

"Stacy the Great," we all said at the same time.

I couldn't help groaning at the thought. It's not exactly a secret that I don't like Stacy Hansen. And it's pretty obvious that she can't stand me, either. It seems like we're always in competition over one thing or another. Katie, Allison, and Randy think she's jealous of me. But I can't understand why.

Anyway, like Randy and Katie said, Stacy probably would end up being our class president. After all, she *is* the most popular girl in seventh grade, her father is the principal of Bradley Junior High . . . and she was sixth-grade class president last year. It was pretty clear that anyone who ran against her didn't have much a chance.

With Stacy running, the election probably wouldn't be very interesting. That was too bad. I had really been looking forward to it.

"Look," said Katie, breaking into my thoughts. She was nodding toward somewhere behind me. "She's starting her campaign already."

I turned my head, and there was Stacy. She was sitting on top of one of the cafeteria tables, flipping her long blond hair and making a speech. Of course, her band of followers was right behind her — B. Z. Latimer, Laurel Spencer, and obnoxious Eva Malone. My friends and I call them the Stacy clones, because they always go along with whatever Stacy does.

I couldn't hear what she was saying, but a lot of kids seemed to be listening. Even my twin brother, Sam, and his best friends, Nick Robbins and Jason McKee, were hanging on every word she said.

"Let's head over there and hear the queen speak," Randy said, getting up from her chair.

"It doesn't look like we'll have to," Katie cut in. "She's coming right this way."

"Oh, brother," I muttered under my breath as I slowly stirred my pineapple yogurt. It made me wish that I had remembered to read my horoscope today. I don't run my life by it or anything, but it sometimes gives helpful hints. Maybe it would have said something like, "Beware of blonds with big mouths. Stay in bed." I laughed at the thought.

". . . and at this time, I'd like to introduce my running mate for vice president, Eva Malone," Stacy was saying in this phony cutesy voice, talking to the kids at the table right next to ours.

"What a surprise," I murmured, getting angrier by the second. "Jaws" Malone flashed her tinfoil smile. Her silver braces are kind of bright, and the glare gets really intense when she's under lights.

"And when I'm class president, I promise to do my best for all of the seventh grade . . ." Stacy went on with another flip of her hair.

I wanted to say something to take the wind out of Stacy's sails. But I couldn't think of what, so I just sat there and listened instead.

"What do you mean, 'when'?" Randy said, suddenly piping in. She was elbowing her way to the front of the small crowd around Stacy. Leave it to Randy! She's better than anyone at making Stacy lose her cool. Randy's not intimidated by anyone or anything. I guess that comes from living in New York City.

"What's that supposed to mean?" Stacy asked in this snooty voice. She put her hands on her hips and squinted her blue eyes at Randy.

"You haven't been elected yet, you know," Randy told her.

"Ha!" Stacy laughed. "As if there's any competition . . ."

I bit down on my plastic spoon so hard, it splintered in my mouth. I was getting angrier by the second.

"Everyone . . . who knows anyone," Stacy went on, "knows that with me running for class president, there's no contest."

"Oohhh, I don't know about that," a voice said. The thing that surprised me was that the voice was coming out of my mouth!

My knees turned to jelly and my tongue felt like it was covered with cotton. But before I knew it I was standing on my chair and my stage voice was booming through the entire cafeteria.

"I, Sabrina Wells, am officially running for class president of the seventh grade!"

I calmly sat back down. I took an unused spoon off of Allison's lunch tray and continued eating my yogurt. Katie, Randy, and Allison just stared at me. I looked up at them and smiled, but kept eating my yogurt. After a while they sat down and we began talking about the election. We decided that the best thing to do was to meet after school at Fitzie's and plan a strategy.

Through this entire conversation, I was still really calm. When the bell rang, though, I sat in my seat suddenly unable to move a muscle. The words *What have you done?* kept echoing through my mind.

Chapter Two

"Sabs, I can't believe what you did today!" Katie squealed as we headed for a booth at Fitzie's, the most popular after-school hangout in Acorn Falls.

"It was totally awesome," Randy agreed. She shrugged off her jacket and sat down next to me, while Katie and Allison slid in on the other side of the table.

"I really admire your nerve," Allison added, smiling. "I could never do a thing like that."

Katie's blue eyes were sparkling as she leaned across the table. "Climbing up on that chair like that! Sabs, that was really a surprise."

"Especially to me!" I exclaimed.

In fact, I was still in total shock. Usually I feel that I have so much to say that I will burst if I don't get it all out. But ever since lunchtime, I hadn't been able to find my voice.

"Did you see Stacy's face?" Randy asked,

starting to laugh. "She looked like she was ready to throw up."

"I felt like I was about to throw up myself," I said. Just thinking about it made me feel a little queasy again.

"Really?" Katie questioned. "You sounded totally confident."

I smiled nervously at her. "Well, I was only pretending — in a big way."

"That's why you're such a good actress," Allison put in.

"But the look on Stacy's face," Randy said again, shaking her head. "If just wish had a camera."

I hadn't even been aware of Stacy's reaction to my announcement. But now that Randy mentioned it, I tried to picture her. A second later I was cracking up. Then we were all laughing hysterically. Somehow that made me feel a lot calmer.

Just then, Stacy walked into Fitzie's with Eva, B.Z., and Laurel following behind her like baby ducks. I watched her stop in the doorway and look around the room until she spotted us. Before I knew it, she had breezed through the crowd and was standing at our table.

"I wanted to wish you luck, Sabrina," Stacy told me sarcastically. "You're definitely going to need it."

With that, she flipped back her blond hair and sauntered to a booth on the other side of the restaurant.

I knew she was just trying to intimidate me. The problem was, it was working. Suddenly I got a lump in my throat. I felt as if I had swallowed a whole cantaloupe or something.

"Are you okay, Sabrina?" Allison asked.

I took a deep breath and started blowing air out of my cheeks. It's this dumb thing I do when I get really anxious.

"You're kind of nervous, aren't you?" Katie guessed, reading my thoughts. I blew out some more air.

Randy draped her arm around my shoulders. "Hey, it's not like you're in this alone," she reminded me. "It's all for one, and one for all!"

"Sure," Allison continued. "We're a team. Even the president of the United States doesn't get elected all by himself."

That was something I hadn't even had time to think about. I was so shocked by the fact that

I was running at all, I had totally forgotten that I have the absolutely best friends in the whole world. I immediately started to feel a lot better.

It suddenly occurred to me that a presidential campaign was almost the same as putting on a show. And what was really cool about this show is that I had the starring role. I was beginning to feel really excited. If I could approach this as an actress, I just knew I'd have the election in the bag.

Okay, so maybe I wasn't very good at politics and organizing and all that, but that's where Katie, Allison, and Randy would come in. I took another deep breath and leaned forward in my seat.

"You're right," I said, smiling. "The very first Sabrina Wells for President campaign Meeting is now in session," I said, banging my fist on the table like a judge's gavel.

"Here, here," Katie stated, pounding the table with her own make-believe gavel.

"Here! Here! Here!" we all said in unison, pounding the table with our fists and cracking up again.

"Is anyone *here* going to order any ice cream today?"

Surprised, we all glanced up to see our waitress standing there. She was holding her pad and looking at us as if we were crazy.

That only made us laugh even more, but we managed to get ourselves enough under control to order some sodas. Then we got to work.

We all agreed that Katie would be perfect as campaign secretary. After all, she has the best penmanship and she is the most organized. Next we appointed Randy my campaign and public relations manager, because next to me, she knows the most people at Bradley. Then we decided that Allison should be the presidential adviser. None of us really knew what that was exactly, but we figured a presidential adviser had to be smart and well informed, two things Al definitely is. I mean, she read over a hundred books last summer.

I started feeling much more confident.

"And as for Eva Malone . . ." I drummed my fingers on the table, thinking out loud.

"That's right," Randy cut in, "we haven't picked a running mate yet. Who's going to run against Eva for vice president?"

I looked at Randy, Randy looked at Allison, Allison looked at Katie, and Katie looked back at me.

"Seems like we're all booked up," Katie said.

"It might be better if Sabs's running mate isn't one of us anyway," Allison pointed out.

Randy nodded. "That's right. As your official campaign manager, I think we should pick someone totally different. Someone who has a different outlook and a different group of friends."

"What about a boy?" Allison suggested.

We all gave her a strange look because Al is usually pretty shy around guys. "No. I really mean it," she went on. "That would add a very special slant to our campaign."

I wasn't sure what she meant by that, but it sounded like a good idea. "But who?" I wondered out loud.

We all thought about that for a minute. "What about Winslow Barton?" Randy eventually suggested as she took a sip of her soda. "He's really smart."

Katie shook her head. "Too intellectual."

Winslow is a real computer nut. He's kind of a bookworm and he dresses sort of weird. But he's a pretty good friend of Randy's and ever since Winslow and I did this project in history together, I started to think he's a nice guy, too. Of course, it's not exactly a secret that he has a giant crush on me. But I agreed with Katie. I couldn't really see him as a vice-presidential candidate.

"Why not?" Randy asked, stirring her soda with her straw.

"I just don't think he's the kind of person who would want to be in the public eye," I said seriously.

"That's true," Randy agreed. "He's a private kind of person."

I leaned my elbows on the table and cupped my chin in the palms of my hands. I really believe that I think better in this position. I sat there, trying to come up with some ideas.

"I think she's waiting for the glue to set so her head doesn't fall off and roll under the table again," I heard an all too familiar voice quip.

"It's a very embarrassing situation," the voice continued. "Her head rolls off her body at least once a day . . ."

I looked up to find my twin brother, Sam, standing beside our table. Sam has the same curly red hair and freckles as I do, but that's about all we have in common. Right now he was laughing with his friends, Nick and Jason , who were standing right behind him.

"Cut it out, Sam," I said, turning in his direction.

"Got room for a couple more?" he asked.

Before I could say no, he and his friends were shoving their way into our tiny booth. There we were. Seven people crammed into a booth for four.

"C'mon, Sam! I'm trying to think," I pleaded, getting more annoyed every second.

"I told you, Sabrina," he began in this phony caring voice, "never attempt to do that all by yourself. It puts too much of a strain on your tiny little brain."

I gave him a shove with my right elbow, and faster than lightning his right hand came out of the blue and playfully bopped me on the head. Without even thinking, I started tweaking his nose between my fingers.

"Honk! Honk!" He started making these awful goose sounds. Then his right hand started bopping me on the head in perfect rhythm with every honk.

Practically everyone in Fitzie's stopped to watch us. All the kids were laughing and clapping as Sam started making all these crazy faces and honking louder than ever. It amazes me sometimes that the two of us are twins. He's totally incapable of being serious. Finally, he stood up and took a bow.

"You two are a riot." Nick said laughing.

Katie managed to stop laughing long enough to add, "You should be a comedy act."

Suddenly I noticed a twinkle in Randy's dark eyes. She was looking at me with this weird expression on her face.

"Yeah, Sabrina," Randy said slowly. "You and Sam really make a great team." I noticed that she put a lot of emphasis on the word *"team."*

All of a sudden I felt a bubble of dread in the pit of my stomach. "Oh, no!" I exclaimed. "I hope you're not thinking what I think you're thinking."

"Of course! That's perfect!" Allison agreed, looking from me to Sam.

"You mean Sam? Sam for vice president? Are you kidding?" I asked. How could they even consider it?

Everyone at the table nodded their head yes — except Sam.

"Sam? Sam for vice president?" he repeated, looking under the table. Then he started looking behind himself.

"Sam? Sam who?" he asked with this innocent look on his red-freckled face.

"Sam you, you goof," Randy stated, pointing her finger right at him.

"Sam me?" he questioned, jabbing his index finger into his chest. "Me Sam?"

"Oh, cut it out! Just cut it out!" I screamed at him. Then I whipped my head around to look at Randy on my other side. "Randy, are you nuts or something?"

"I think it's a great idea," Katie chimed in eagerly.

"I agree," Allison said very seriously. "He's funny, he's popular, and he knows all the jocks, so he can pull in a lot of votes that Stacy and Eva couldn't even hope to pull in." She was counting the reasons off on her fingers. "Most of the boys in the seventh grade will probably vote for you guys just because there's a guy running on the ticket."

"And votes are what it's all about," Randy

added, looking at me for an answer.

I took a deep breath. I had a feeling I was going to be taking a lot of deep breaths during this campaign. Then I looked at Sam. He was holding his side and doing his "silent laugh." You know, the kind where you're cracking up so hard that no sound comes out.

"If I agree to this, are you going to take this campaign seriously?" I asked him.

He just laughed some more. "Sam, I'm talking to you!" I bellowed, putting my face right up to his.

Sam's smile vanished, and for a split second I actually thought I was going to get a serious, straight answer.

"Sabrina," he began quietly. "If you really want me to be your running mate for president, I can only answer it in one simple word . . ."

He grabbed my nose and honked loudly. Then he sprang from his seat, squatted down on the floor, shoved his hands into his armpits, and waddled out of Fitzie's like a duck, honking every step of the way.

He had the whole place in stitches. I was getting more embarrassed by the second, and I could feel my body blush coming on.

This is who they wanted for my running mate? Sam the duck-man? I couldn't believe it. But, boy, does news travel fast in a place like Fitzie's.

Within seconds, everyone seemed to be talking about me and Sam. Kids started coming up to me and asking if we were really running together.

"Shake their hands," Randy whispered into my ear. "You're a candidate now. You have to act like one. Just smile and shake everyone's hand."

I took a deep breath and smiled the biggest smile I could muster. I tried to remember what I had seen candidates do on commercials on TV.

"Sure, Sam and I are running for president and vice president," I muttered. "Vote for us!" I was smiling so hard, my teeth were beginning to ache.

Suddenly, there was a commotion at the other side of the room.

"That's right," I heard Stacy's sickly sweet voice singing high above the crowd.

"Ice-cream cones for everyone. It's on me. Any flavor you want. Just don't forget, Stacy

Hansen for president. I know you'll remember my name." She laughed.

Stacy turned to shoot me a dirty look from across the room. Then she plastered her dazzling fake smile back on.

I watched kids gather around Stacy and Eva up at the soda fountain. That old sinking feeling came back into my stomach. Ice cream for everyone? How would Sam and I ever be able to compete with that?

Chapter Three

I could not believe that Sam and I were running against Stacy Hansen and Eva Malone for president and vice president of the seventh grade. I could not believe I had actually let my friends talk me into it. But by the time we left Fitzie's, I knew there was no turning back. Everyone was talking about it.

As I walked home I was glad for the cold, brisk air. It helped clear my head — a little, anyway. When I got to my house, I went straight to my room. The best thing about my whole life is my room. It's in the attic so it's very private, and it has the coolest sloping ceilings. Having it is definitely the biggest advantage to being the only girl out of five kids.

Sitting down on my bed, I went over the events of the day. I was so confused. And when I'm really confused, the only thing that clears my mind is putting a blanket over my head.

I'm not sure why, but it usually works.

So I sat there with this blanket over my head and tried to think. But after about five minutes, it got really hot under there and I didn't feel any better. Jumping up, I started to pace around the room. That's what they always do in the movies.

If I could just find a way to get Sam to take this campaign seriously, we might pull it off. I suddenly stopped pacing as I realized that I had two campaigns on my hands. One was running for class president, and the other was getting Sam to start acting like a human being. I figured I had a better chance of becoming the first woman president of the United States than getting Sam to act serious.

Then I remembered what my music teacher, Mr. Metcalf, told us about playing in the school band. Sometimes — well most of the time — I don't practice my clarinet enough. Mr. Metcalf always says, "If you want this band to be taken seriously, you have to take yourselves seriously."

That's what I had to do. I had to show Sam how serious I was about winning this election. I had to be confident and motivated at all times!

I had to *act* like a winner, so I could *be* a winner!

Feeling more hopeful, I lay back on my bed again and started looking around my room. My eyes stopped at the opposite wall, which is full of posters of all my favorite movie stars and rock bands. I noticed a magazine cover I'd cut out, of Sylvester Stallone. He's one of my idols. Not only does he act, but he writes and directs all the movies he stars in, like Rambo and *Rocky*.

Suddenly a great idea struck me. I leaned over and rummaged through my cassette drawer until I found the perfect tape. It was the theme from the first Rocky movie. I popped it into my Walkman, and put on my earphones.

"Da-da-da-da-da-da-DA-da-da-da . . ." the trumpets blared. I couldn't keep still. Jumping up, I started marching around the room. Every time I hear that song, it makes me think of how Rocky always wins the fight — against all odds.

It was kind of like Stacy and me. I just knew she was going to stage a flashy and expensive campaign. There was no way I could start giving out ice-cream cones to the world. Stacy

Hansen was going to buy votes. So I had to use my imagination, my smarts, to come up with a solid campaign that the other kids would get excited about. I puffed up my chest and reminded myself that I had to "use my guts," just like Rocky.

"Keep your eye on the prize," I said to myself. I turned up the volume full blast and started marching to the beat.

"'Riding high now! Gonna try now! Gonna fly . . . Flyyy,'" I started singing along. I could feel myself getting excited! Confident! And more importantly, the theme from *Rocky* always makes me feel American! I marched even faster, reminding myself that I would have to be in tip-top shape for the campaign. I promised myself to exercise every day. And absolutely no more junk food until the campaign was over!

As the tape neared the end I started to get ready for the big finale. I ran in place, and then threw my arms up and out in a sign of victory, just like Rocky!

I felt totally exhilarated. I had my secret weapon. It would be my theme song for the whole campaign. I vowed to listen to it at least three times a day and play it at the beginning of every campaign meeting. It would be my "motivational theme song." And right now, it was just what I needed to get ready to work on Sam.

It wasn't until my mother called me for dinner that I realized how much time had passed. I flew downstairs, but stopped short at the foot of the stairs.

"If you want to be taken seriously, you have to take yourself seriously." Mr. Metcalf's words echoed in my mind.

I took a deep breath and straightened my back, making sure to walk erect. I had to approach the dining room in a dignified manner.

With my head held high, I made my first entrance as "Sabrina Wells, presidential candidate." Confident and smiling.

"Evening," I announced, taking my seat.

Everyone else was already at the table. Except for my oldest brother, Matt, that is. He's away at college. I could see my parents exchange a look. Sam and my older brothers Mark and Luke were rolling their eyes at me. But I ignored them. Just because they weren't going to take me seriously didn't mean I wasn't going to. I shook out my napkin and placed it on my lap.

While Mom mixed up the large bowl of spaghetti and meatballs, I looked at Sam, wondering if he would say anything about our running for seventh-grade president and vice president. But when he caught my glance, he just started whistling and looking around the room.

Obviously, it was up to me. I sat up straight in my seat, getting ready to make the big announcement.

"Sam, the dinner table is not the place for whistling," my mother scolded him before I could open my mouth. She placed a dish of the steaming hot pasta in front of me, and I looked at it nervously.

How was I supposed to eat spaghetti in a dignified manner? It didn't seem possible. I tried pretending I was at a dinner at the White House. As daintily as I could, I poked my fork into the mound of pasta and picked up two tiny strands.

"What's the matter, Sabs?" Mark asked, crinkling up his nose. "Something wrong with your spaghetti?"

"Tastes great to me," Sam cut in, filling his mouth with a giant forkful.

"No, no. It's wonderful," I assured him. I looked at Mom and flashed her my candidate smile.

Sam was busy stuffing another giant forkful of spaghetti and meatballs into his mouth before he'd even had a chance to swallow the first. He smiled at me and started chomping down even faster. He looked like a pig. Turning him into a serious vice-presidential candidate was going to be even harder than I thought!

"Sabrina, you look like you have some big news," Mom said after everyone had been served. "Are you going to share it with the rest of us?"

I carefully put down my fork and folded my hands in front of me. "Well, now that you've asked, I do have some big news," I began. "I've decided to run for class president."

I blinked my eyes a few times, waiting for a reaction.

"That's wonderful," Dad replied. At the same time, Mom grinned and said, "Congratulations!"

"Good for you, Sabs," Luke told me. He

even stopped eating to applaud. Luke's like that. Most of the time he acts like he's twelve instead of sixteen. But every once in a while, he behaves like a grown-up. He really seemed happy for me.

Even Mark joined in and started to clap and whistle. But Sam was still busy chewing his huge mouthful of spaghetti. I knew he was doing it on purpose, but I decided not to pay any attention.

"So, who's your running mate?" Mark asked, as if he didn't already know. Mark's only a year ahead of Sam and me at Bradley, and I could tell by the fake-innocent way he was asking that Sam had already told him.

I looked straight at my twin brother. Sam just kept chewing, his cheeks full of food. I took a deep breath.

"Samuel," I announced.

Sam's hazel eyes widened. In one split second, it was as if he had exploded, sending a mouthful of spaghetti, tomatoes, and cheese straight for me! I ducked under the table for cover, but it was too late. My face and shirt were plastered with pasta and sauce.

"Samuel!" he repeated, laughing and choking all at once. Mark and Luke started patting him on the back and laughing hysterically. Obviously, they thought that having their sister covered with spaghetti was the funniest thing in the whole world.

I could feel a lump welling up in my throat. I tried to control myself, but I couldn't. I felt totally humiliated. My eyes filled with tears.

"Sam, you're disgusting!" I shouted. Then I bolted from the table, heading straight for the shower. Behind me, I could hear Mom yelling at Sam, and suddenly the laughter died down.

"Oh, I hope he gets into loads of trouble," I murmured under my breath as I peeled off my gooey clothes and turned on the water full blast. Randy and her bright ideas. Sam for vice president. Forget it! There was just no way this was going to work!

After my shower, I put on some jeans and a soft aqua sweatshirt. I was dying to call Katie. I didn't feel like facing anyone at the table and I'd have to go downstairs to use the phone. I wasn't crying anymore, but I still felt pretty miserable. All I could do was lie on my bed and stare at the ceiling.

A few minutes later, I heard footsteps coming up the stairs. I could tell it was Sam. No one else in our family stomps their shoes as loudly as he does. He was the last person in the world I wanted to talk to. I shut my eyes to make it look like I was asleep. My family says I can be very melodramatic.

The door creaked open, and I heard Sam come in and kneel beside my bed.

"I know you're not asleep, Sabrina," he whispered.

I kept my eyes shut and concentrated hard, figuring it was good practice for acting on a soap opera. Sometimes the characters are in a hospital bed for months. I used to think about how easy it would be to go to work and just lie down. Until now, I had no idea how hard it really is.

"C'mon, Sabs, wake up," Sam said, nudging my shoulder. "I'm sorry. I came to tell you I'm sorry."

I didn't budge. All I wanted was for him to go away. Suddenly, I felt a tickling sensation on my nose. I tried to remain still, but I couldn't resist peeking through my eyelids.

"I sur . . . rennder," he sang as the tickling continued. I could see the blur of a white flag made from a T-shirt he had attached to one of Mom's long wooden spoons. He kept waving the flag over my nose.

"I'm sorrr-y," he repeated in the same sing-song way. I tried not to breathe, even though I was having this incredible urge to scratch my nose.

"I know you're faking it," Sam continued, lowering the flag to somewhere near my bare foot. I couldn't control myself. My feet are incredibly ticklish.

I leapt to my feet, causing Sam to jump back in surprise.

"Cut it out, Sam!" I yelled. "Just leave me alone! You don't have to run for vice president. Just go away!"

"C'mon, Sabrina. I said I was sorry. I'm ready to get serious." Sam clasped his hands together and gave me his most angelic smile.

"Really?" I questioned, shooting him a dubious look.

"Really!"

"Because you want to?" I asked.

" . . . Yeah . . . yes!" he hesitantly replied.

My eyes narrowed suspiciously as I asked, "How come?"

"Be-because . . . I want to," he stuttered. He was smiling weakly and waving his makeshift flag in my face. But I wasn't about to fall for his act.

Glaring at him, I shot back, "And because Mom said you have to! Right?"

"Okay, okay. That's part of it," Sam admitted.

"I knew it! I never should have — "

"But that's not all of it," he jumped in, cutting me off. "I really do want to run for vice president."

This time, he actually sounded like he meant it. "Why?" I asked again.

Sam stopped and thought for a moment. "Because . . . I care about Bradley and I think that we could make a difference. And . . . I know how much you want to win," he said slowly. "And I think I can help."

Shyly, he turned his face away. I couldn't believe it! Sam was actually blushing! I mean, Sam can fake a lot of things, but there is no way he can fake a body blush. Maybe he really could get serious.

Slowly, he turned back to me and waved his flag. "Truce?"

I made sure to pause a moment before I answered. "Truce. But you have to swear that you'll start behaving like a serious candidate."

He put his flag down, looked at the floor, and thrust his hands deep into his pockets. Then he pulled out something that looked like a rumpled napkin. He began to unwrap it. I couldn't believe it. It was a meatball! He placed it on my night table and laid his hand over it.

"I, Samuel Wells . . ." he announced dramatically, emphasizing the word "Samuel."

". . . do solemnly swear, that from this moment on, I will stop acting like a meatball and start behaving like a serious person."

Then he flashed me a big grin, picked up the meatball, and took a big bite.

"This is the meatball of truth," he seriously informed me as he stuffed the rest in his mouth.

Chapter Four

I woke up Wednesday morning, not sure whether Sam was serious about running for vice president or not. But I decided I didn't have the time to worry about it. There was just too much to do. Anyway, I know for a fact that the best way to get Sam not to do something is to ask him to do it. And the best way to get him to do something is to act like it doesn't matter. So I figured that's what I would do. Just act like it didn't matter.

I got up extra early and pulled my gym shorts on over my pajamas. Then I put on my sneakers and a sweatband. Exercising before breakfast! Now that's discipline, I thought to myself.

Turning on my cassette deck, I started doing warm-up stretches to "Rocky," my motivational theme song. Then I rummaged through my closet, looking for something "presidential" to wear. I knew that Stacy was probably going to get a whole new wardrobe. But there was no way my mom would let me do that. I had to find a way to put something great together with what I had.

But before I started on my clothes, I decided I'd better work on my hair. I read an article that said that the right hairstyle can make or break an outfit, and I really believe that's true.

I started by parting my hair on one side, thinking I might look older that way. But my hair's so thick and curly, it kept springing back to the middle. Next I tried piling it on top of my head for a more sophisticated look, but it made my face look too fat. Finally, I just pulled it back into a bun.

Now for my clothes. I decided to mix some of my skirts and tops for a red, white, and blue theme. But when I looked at myself in the mirror, I wasn't sure if I liked it. All I needed was a needle and thread and I would look like Betsy Ross! The bun definitely had to go.

I undid my bun and shook my curls free. After staring at myself in the mirror, I tried tying my hair back in a low ponytail. It kind of made me look like Paul Revere. On second thought, I decided I liked it. Patriotic, without being too severe. I fumbled in my dresser drawer for a black ribbon, which I tied in a bow around my auburn curls. Perfect! Black and orange, just like Bradley's school colors.

That gave me an even better idea. If I was going to be patriotic, I figured it should be to Bradley Junior High. Instead of red, white, and blue, I'd wear black and orange.

Finding a black skirt was easy, but I didn't have any solid orange tops. I would have to settle for something with other colors that had some orange in it. Finally, I found an old cotton blouse that had a vegetable print on it. There were eggplants and tomato vines all over it. The eggplants were a little on the purple side, but I figured they could pass for black. And the tomatoes were an orang-y shade of red. It would just have to do.

Then I remembered the perfect thing to complete the outfit. I had a pair of orange tights left over from a school play, back in fifth grade. I had played a chicken in a production of *Li'l Abner.* That was before I got really serious about acting.

I dug the tights from the back of my drawer,

then I wiggled into them. Most of the time I feel so short, compared to everyone else in the seventh grade, that I hadn't realized how much I'd grown in the past few years. The tights just barely reached my waist, but I decided I could live with them.

Shoes were another story, though. My only black ones were too summery to wear now. And there was no way I could wear a black-and-orange outfit with my brown school shoes. The only thing I had in black were my snow boots. They weren't the greatest, but at least they matched the skirt.

I didn't really have any more time to fuss. Running downstairs, I grabbed a piece of toast, threw on my jacket, grabbed my bookbag, and headed out the door. I couldn't believe how late it was. No matter how early I get up, I always seem to be rushing to school without a minute to spare.

The first bell was ringing when I got to the school's main door. Being late for class on my first day as a presidential candidate wouldn't look too good. I pulled open the door and started running down the hallway.

But having my snow boots on didn't help.

They're kind of clumsy, and I had to waddle just so I wouldn't trip. I must've looked like an orange-and-black penguin, or something. Some presidential candidate! To make matters worse, it felt like my orange tights were slipping down. I was feeling totally frustrated.

If it hadn't been for Sam, I would've planned my outfit the night before and not be in this mess! The day had just started and I was mad at him already!

Luckily, I made it to my seat in math class in the nick of time. The morning went by without any more catastrophes. But it was pretty clear from the looks on my friends' faces that my outfit wasn't a big hit.

"You look like a vegetable garden," Randy joked as we walked down the hall toward the cafeteria after English.

I explained about wearing the school's colors and my Bradley patriotic theme, but I don't think the message was getting across. Maybe it was all those eggplants.

"You and Sam seem to be taking very different approaches to this campaign," Allison commented.

In my rush to get to school, I had totally

forgotten about Sam. "What are you talking about?" I asked, feeling very confused.

Randy looked at me with wide eyes. "Are you telling me that you had nothing to do with Sam's outfit?" she asked.

"I was running so late this morning, I didn't even get a chance to see Sam," I answered. I was getting more and more worried.

"I really didn't think he was going to go for this campaigning routine," Katie chimed in without answering my question. "I couldn't believe the way he was carrying on this morning."

"He looked pretty cute. But the two of you better get together and settle on one theme," Randy cut in. "We'll have to have a meeting pretty soon. There's no way we can work on your speeches for the special election rally until we decide on a campaign strategy."

Now I was really getting scared. "What?" I practically screamed at my best friends. "What is he doing? What in the world are you talking about?" I ran as fast as I could the rest of the way to the cafeteria — which wasn't very fast in my boots.

The first people I saw when I got there were

Stacy Hansen and Eva Malone. They had a small crowd around them. And of course Stacy was wearing a new outfit. It was this blue double-breasted blazer with gold stripes on the sleeves and the lapels. She wore it over a matching skirt with a gold stripe around the hem.

I was too worried about Sam to pay too much attention to her, but I couldn't help noticing that the outfit made Stacy look sort of like an admiral in the navy.

The other side of the cafeteria was so full, I couldn't even see what was going on. I pushed through the crowd to see what was happening. Suddenly I stopped short. I could not believe my eyes.

There was my brother Sam — my silly, funny, wonderful brother Sam, dressed in his blue-striped baseball pants and a red shirt. On top of his head was a huge cardboard top hat with a cartoon cutout of Uncle Sam pasted on it above the words UNCLE SAM WANTS YOU TO VOTE WELLS, in bold red, white, and blue letters.

I couldn't believe it. He must have spent half the night working on that hat. And he had done it for me. I could almost hear my "Rocky" motivational theme song playing in the background. Now I was sure we could win.

Sam spotted me and flashed our secret wink. I was so happy, I felt like crying. I couldn't believe it. Sam was finally on my team! My heart felt like it was going to burst with pride. It was one of the greatest moments of my life.

Out of the corner of my eye, I saw Stacy Hansen and her gang heading straight for me. She walked up to me with her hands on her hips. But this time, I was ready for her.

"So, you and your brother think you're really cool, don't you?" Stacy began, glancing at the crowd.

Facing her, I put my hands on my hips in the same determined way she had. "We are cool," I told her firmly. "And we are going to win this election."

"You think so?" she questioned with a flip of her hair.

"I know so," I answered.

Stacy squinted her eyes at me, then said, "Well, this means war."

And people say I'm dramatic. "You really

scare me, Stacy," I shot back, rolling my eyes.

"You should be scared, Sabrina. Because there's no way you and Sam are winning this election," Eva added, stepping up beside Stacy.

"Says who?" Randy challenged. I glanced over my shoulder and saw that she, Al, and Katie had formed a semicircle behind me.

When I looked back at Stacy, she was holding something up in front of my face. "Says this!"

I just looked at the thing for a second. "You're gonna win the election with a ball, point pen?" I asked skeptically.

"By next week's rally, this pen is going to say 'Stacy Hansen for President' on it," Stacy went on in this snide voice. "And every kid in our class is going to have one!"

"And that's just the beginning," Laurel chimed in.

"What are you guys giving out?" Eva asked obnoxiously.

For a second I just stared at Stacy. I mean, candidates were supposed to win elections based on their ideas and spirit and dedication, right? I had lots of those things. But I have to admit it — I was jealous. What if everyone fell for her Santa Claus act? We wouldn't stand a chance!

I felt kind of dumb just standing there, so I was relieved when Katie shouted back, "We're not telling. We don't give out trade secrets."

"Yeah! It's a surprise," Randy added.

I took a deep breath and rolled my eyes.

Yeah, it's a surprise all right, I thought to myself. It was such a big surprise that even *we* didn't know what it was!

Chapter Five

I decided to walk home alone after school to give myself more time to think. The election was just two weeks away and we hadn't even started planning our campaign. And there was the big rally *and* the debate to think about, too.

During lunch we decided to have our first official campaign meeting at Al's house the following day after school. Everyone agreed that we needed to come up with a good strategy before Stacy totally dazzled everyone.

It was hard to concentrate on school the next day because my head was buzzing with thoughts of the election. Naturally, my last-period science class seemed like it would never end. When it was finally over, I ran to my locker for my jacket and hurried out of school ahead of my friends.

I wanted to run home and get something

before meeting them at Allison's. I thought it would be a good idea to have a gavel to call the meeting to order. We didn't have an official one. I didn't think anyone else on the campaign staff had one either. But I was sure I could find a substitute.

When I got home, breathless, I rummaged around the kitchen. After a few minutes I found my mom's big wooden kitchen hammer. She uses it to pound chicken into cutlets. It didn't exactly look official, but at least it was the right shape. I shoved it in my bookbag along with my "Rocky" tape.

By the time I got to Allison's, Sam, Katie, Al, and Randy were already in the Clouds' kitchen, munching on some potato chips. Sam had worn his Uncle Sam hat to school again, and he still had it on. Seeing it made me even more excited about the campaign.

When we went into the dining room, I saw that one end of the table was neatly set with five pads and pencils. Allison's six-year-old brother, Charlie, was sitting at the other end with a coloring book and crayons.

"This is totally great," I said, grinning. "Obviously my campaign team is psyched!"

They looked around at each other with big grins on their faces. I had decided on the way to Al's that the best way for me to get inspired was to inspire my team. I was pleased to see it working. I couldn't help wondering, though, when would be a good time to play my motivational theme song. I wasn't sure Al's parents would appreciate blaring music, so I decided to wait a while before I played it.

"Yeah, Allison got everything set up before we got here," Sam explained as he grabbed a big handful of potato chips.

Randy went to the chair at the head of the table and said in an official voice, "Okay, okay, let's get started."

I sat down and pulled the gavel from my bookbag.

"A gavel! Cool," Randy exclaimed as I passed it to Sam to give to her.

"Smells like garlic," Sam commented, putting it up to his nose.

Charlie looked up from his coloring book and giggled.

"Just pass it on, Sam," Randy said, holding out her hand.

"Should I put that comment into the minutes?" Katie questioned, referring to her notes.

Randy shook her head. "Not necessary."

"Unless we're going to make chicken cutlet parmigiana," Sam joked.

We all started to laugh, but Randy tapped the gavel on the table. "Let's get serious, folks. The rally is next Friday. We've got a lot of work to do if we're going to get Sam and Sabrina elected. This meeting is now in session."

I felt great as I looked around the table. My staff had everything under control. I was sure we'd come up with a great campaign.

"The first thing we have to do is decide what platform our candidates are going to stand on," Randy began, referring to her list.

"I'd like my platform to be . . . the bleachers in the gym," Sam interrupted. "They're easy to stand on. And, besides that, I'll look taller than everyone else."

Allison and Katie burst out laughing, but I didn't think it was funny. So much for Sam's promise to get serious. But at least they all stopped laughing when Randy pounded the gavel again.

"Not that kind of platform," Allison blurted out, stifling a last giggle. "What would you like your political platform to be?"

"I think the first thing we should do is figure out what Stacy's platform is," Katie commented. Leave it to Katie to take the logical approach.

Allison nodded. "Yes. Then we can work with it . . . find a way to improve it. We'll have to use every strategy we can."

Obviously Al was reading up on everything she could for this campaign. It made me feel great to know that my best friends were all working so hard for Sam and me.

"Well, what has Stacy been talking about?" I asked. "Who's been listening to her speeches?"

"I have," Sam said, raising his hand in a very professional manner. He leaned forward in his chair, rubbing his chin with his hand as he said, "It seems to me that Stacy Hansen's platform is to get every girl at Bradley to learn to blow-dry her hair exactly the right way — every day."

Even I had to laugh at that.

"The only other strategy I can see she has," Katie put in, "is giving out tons of freebies." She tapped her pencil dejectedly on her pad, adding, "And there's no way we can match her."

"Well, maybe that's true," Randy went on. "But we can't let that get us down."

"Right!" I cried. I had been thinking about that since Stacy had waved her stupid pen in my face.

"We have to deal with the issues. We have to let the students know that there are things Sam and I can do for Bradley that Stacy isn't even considering. I mean, just because she gave out free pens doesn't mean she cares about the seventh grade. We can show people that we do care."

Our meeting lasted for an hour and a half. When we were done, we had our ideas all set up for next week's rally. Katie, our efficient secretary, summed it up and read it out loud.

"Okay, Sabrina and Sam's platform is as follows. The main idea that they'll have to keep in mind is that the Wells team is serious about Bradley . . . and Stacy is not."

She went on to read our ideas. We had really put a lot of thought into them, and, I had to admit, we had come up with some great ideas. First we decided that, except for the annual ski trip, most of our class trips were pretty boring, so that was something that needed changing. Sam really surprised me with the next idea. He pointed out that the gym equipment was old and worn out. So we decided that better gym equipment would be our second improvement. But we were really at a loss as to what else needed improvement. Leave it to good old Al to come up with something. She suggested better library books. She thought a lot of kids would read more if they had more current stuff to read. Brilliant!

We all clapped when Katie finished reading the list.

"Next order of business," Randy said loudly, using her gavel again. She consulted her list. "We have to have a poster-making meeting A S A P"

"A.S.A.P.?" we all muttered.

"As soon as possible," she informed us.

Randy's father produces commercials and rock videos, and Randy used to work with him sometimes before she and her mom moved here from New York City. That must be where she picked up expressions like "A S A P"

"But, Randy, we're not allowed to put up posters until the week of the election," Al pointed out. "That's the week after next."

We finally decided to have the poster meeting at my house the weekend after the rally. When Sam, Katie, Randy, and I left Al's house, I was really excited. I didn't know how I was going to be able to wait until next Friday's rally!

Chapter Six

The week flew by. On Friday, the day of the rally, I woke up super early. I was excited and nervous at the same time. I checked everything three times over before I left the house. But I still had the feeling that something was missing.

We had decided to stay with the red, white, and blue theme since it had worked so well for Sam. I chose a navy dress with a red cardigan sweater over it. I was sure that Stacy was going to wear something flashy, but I decided to stick with the simple look. It had worked so far. I rummaged around for a navy ribbon for my hair. Then I remembered it was in the bathroom, so I trooped back down the attic stairs to get it. Sam was wearing his good jeans, a white shirt, a red tie, and, of course, his Uncle Sam hat. Even Randy, Katie, and Allison were dressing in red, white, and blue.

"Let's Get Serious About Bradley" was our theme. I hoped it would work.

The rally was being held in the gym right before lunch, instead of third-period English. Naturally, I had gotten to my classes at the last minute, so I didn't get a chance to talk to any of my friends until after band class.

Katie and I have band together, so while I was putting my clarinet in its case, Katie came over to me. She was wearing red corduroy pants, a white angora sweater, and her blue headband.

"Wow, you look great. Have you seen Stacy yet?" I asked in a rush. "I can't believe we're going to give a speech in front of the whole seventh grade. What's she wearing? Does she have any more freebies?"

"I haven't seen her yet," Katie said, answering my question. "Don't worry about her, Sabs. You and Sam are going to do great."

We hurried to our locker, and I threw my clarinet case into the jumble of my stuff at the bottom. Katie tucked her flute neatly on top of her books on the shelf above. I would definitely have to get around to cleaning my half of our locker after this election.

I straightened out my navy bow, took a deep breath, and we headed for the gym. My speech was written down on notepaper, and I took the sheets out of the pocket of my jeans skirt. I glanced through to make sure I knew every single word by heart, even though I knew I did.

Stacy, Eva, B.Z., and Laurel were already in the gym when we got there. They were all decked out in orange "Stacy for President" T-shirts that had a giant computerized picture of Stacy on the front. When they turned around there was a tiny picture of Eva on the back. I couldn't help wondering if Eva cared that her picture was so small.

The rest of their outfits were pretty good, too. They were wearing black leggings with orange-and-black-striped leg warmers. They were all handing out "Stacy for President" pens. I must admit they looked fantastic.

Stacy shot me a smug smile from across the gym and flipped her long blond hair over her shoulder. I started blowing air nervously out of my cheeks. I looked at Sam, and he just shrugged his shoulders and gave me his "what can you do?" look. Even Katie, Randy, and Al looked a little worried.

The rally was in fifteen minutes! Stacy's team looked outrageous, and here were Sam and I looking like Mr. and Mrs. Ben Franklin! I kept thinking of what Stacy had told me last week in the cafeteria: This means war. Boy, she hadn't been kidding.

"Good luck, Sabs," said a voice to my left. I looked over to see Winslow Barton. He was carrying a clipboard with the words OPINION POLL written across the top.

"I guess we don't have to look at that to figure out which candidates the voters favor," Sam mumbled, peering over Winslow's shoulder.

"I'm getting some feedback for my article in the *Bradley Banner*," Winslow explained. "Care to hear some comments about your opposition?" He pushed his glasses up on the bridge of his nose and flipped back a few pages.

"And I quote," he began. Then he read from the clipboard:

"'Stacy's experience speaks for itself. I think she'd make a great class president.'"

I felt a sinking sensation in the pit of my stomach. I started to turn away, but Winslow grabbed my arm. "Wait, there's more." He continued to read:

"'Nice outfits, but that doesn't mean I'd vote for them.'

"'I think they look like orange bumble bees.'"

""I hope they give out CDs next week, there's a new disk I've been meaning to buy.'"

"What do you think, Sabrina?" he asked, pushing his glasses up on his nose and staring at me.

I was definitely surprised. I had been sure that we were sunk. But after hearing Winslow's opinion poll, it looked like we still had a fighting chance. My mind started racing a mile a minute.

Stacy had pens . . . but we had a platform. Stacy had outfits . . . but we had our speeches ready. Stacy had everything . . . but we had . . . Then it hit me like a bolt of lightning. We had music! "Rocky," my motivational theme song. It could save the rally! Nothing gets a crowd going like music. That gave me a great idea.

"Katie! Sam! Please go and find Al and Randy and be ready for an emergency meeting in five minutes. Winslow, come with me!"

Chapter Seven

My friends were all looking at me like I was crazy, but I didn't have time to explain. Grabbing Winslow's arm, I ran straight for Mr. Metcalf, who was standing at the front of the gym. He was in charge of the rally, since Mr. Hansen and the vice principal were away for some kind of Board of Education meeting today. That was a lucky thing as far as I was concerned, since what I was about to ask for wasn't strictly allowable.

"Winslow, if we get permission from Mr. Metcalf, is there any way you could hook up my Walkman to the PA system?" I asked, pulling my Walkman out of my bookbag.

"Sure," he replied. "That's simple. We could just clip your headphones over the microphone for the PA. system in the main office. Then it would play throughout the school. It's easy!"

"Winslow Barton, you're a genius!" There was no way I would ever have been able to figure that out. I felt like hugging him.

I get along pretty well with Mr. Metcalf, but it still took a few minutes before he gave us permission. He kept saying that maybe it wasn't fair to Stacy since she didn't seem to have plans for music. Finally I convinced him. I told him it was an election and it was *our* idea to have music, and that I couldn't help it if Stacy didn't think of it. That did it, and he gave us permission. I also convinced him to let us borrow the American flag and the Bradley Junior High School banner we use at football games. After Mr. Metcalf used the gym teacher's phone to call the administration office, Winslow took off with my Walkman and the "Rocky" tape to set everything up.

Great! My plan was working! Now I had to get everyone else ready. Sam and my friends were waiting by the gym doors. I told them my plan.

Just when I was sure that everything was set, Winslow dashed into the room.

"What's wrong?" I asked, seeing his worried expression.

"Sabrina, the microphone is too thin to hold the earphones, and they keep slipping off," he explained.

I resisted the urge to panic and tried to think logically. "Well, can't you just hold them in place?" I asked.

"But then I'll miss the beginning of the rally," he said, frowning. "I need to watch you and Sam, so I can take pictures for the school paper. There's no way I can write an article and get pictures if I'm not there to see anything!"

I took a deep breath and let it out. Great! I thought to myself. How was he going to hold the microphone and be in the gym at the same time? On top of that, I had a feeling that if Winslow wrote an article for the *Banner*, it would probably help our campaign.

But it was too late to get anybody else to help out. The whole class was in the gym. Anyway, I didn't feel I could trust anyone else. It might ruin the surprise. I gulped when I saw the gym clock. I had less than nine minutes before the rally began! I looked frantically around the room for an idea. Then it struck me.

"Mr. Metcalf?" I said, running up to him again. "One more favor?"

"What is it, Sabrina?" he asked, taking a deep breath. "Would you like me to turn the whole school over to you and Sam?"

Adopting my most presidential expression, I said, "The first aid kit. Can we borrow the first aid kit?"

"Expecting a lot of casualties from this campaign?" he asked with a smile.

"Please," I begged, clasping my hands together.

I could tell he was trying to look stern. But at last he just sighed and said, "Okay, Sabrina."

Luckily there's a first aid kit right in the gym, so it only took a second for Mr. Metcalf to get it. "Here you go," he said, handing it to me. "But make sure you note everything you use on the inventory list. It's very important that the kit's ready to use at . . ."

I didn't even give him a chance to finish his sentence. I went flying down the hallway, the kit in my hands, with Winslow at my heels. Less than five minutes to go. As soon as we reached the main office, I fumbled with the clasp and opened the box.

"Phew!" I muttered under my breath. An open box of gauze bandages was right on top. Good. I wouldn't have to search. Every second counted.

"Sabrina, what on earth . . ." Winslow began. But he quickly figured out what I was doing as I began to unroll the gauze. He let out a low whistle.

"And you say I'm a genius," he commented admiringly.

I held the earphones around the microphone and began wrapping the roll of gauze around it. Now they would stay in place without anyone there to hold them. Within seconds my invention began looking like a giant broken thumb. Winslow and I both cracked up at the sight. The office secretary looked skeptical, but she didn't say anything.

After a few seconds, Winslow took the gauze from me and said, "Get going. I'll finish."

"Don't forget to put some tape around it for good measure," I added, flying out of the room.

Suddenly I stopped right in my tracks. Who would turn off the tape recorder when the song ended? I ran back to the secretary and explained the problem. She didn't say anything but stared at me over the tops of her glasses. Then she flashed me this really weird smile and gave me the thumbs up sign. I took that to mean that she would help me out and I went running out of the room a second time.

As I raced back to the gym I finally figured out what was missing from my campaign. It was me! I had become so involved in having a campaign staff, I had forgotten all about the Sabrina Wells Creative Magic. But it was all coming back to me. I started to feel that backstage tingling I always get before I go on stage.

I checked to see that everyone was at their stations. Sam and I stood at the back of the gym and watched Stacy and her team do this rap song. The song didn't even rhyme in the right places. But as they got into it, all the kids started clapping to the beat:

"If you want a good school president,
And you want it one, two, three
Then you better vote for Hansen.
Stacy! Stacy! Stacy!"

Everybody clapped when they were finished. But I couldn't believe that Stacy didn't bother to make a speech. I guess she figured her song said it all. Talk about being stuck-up!

After the clapping died down, people started looking around. I could tell that no one could figure out why Sam and I weren't up on the bleacher platform with Stacy. It was time to start!

I stood back and motioned to Katie and Randy to take their positions at the entrance of the gym. They had already unrolled the huge rectangular Bradley banner and stood at opposite ends holding it up.

Sam took his place behind them and started to wave the flag. Between his hat and his outfit, he looked kind of like a toy soldier. But a really cute toy soldier.

As I took my place behind Sam, Allison ran down the hall to give Winslow the signal to start the music. It couldn't have worked out any better if we had rehearsed it a million times.

A hush came over the crowd as the first sounds of the trumpets echoed through the room. Every head in the place turned to face the doorway as Katie and Randy walked through the gym, holding the Bradley banner.

The music blared. Everyone started cheering as Sam marched down the aisle, waving the flag and saluting. The "Rocky" theme went into full blast just as I made my entrance, clasping my hands together over my head in a sign of victory.

The crowd went wild and started clapping and hooting their approval. When we got to the bleacher platform, I stole a glance at Stacy. She looked furious.

Sam went first, beginning his speech by shouting out, "Are you ready to get serious about Bradley Junior High?"

The reply was a resounding "Yes!"

"Then you must be ready to vote for us!" He kept on repeating this until he worked the whole school into a frenzy. And then, just at the right moment, he began his speech.

I couldn't believe how good he was. Even though we had gone over all the points at our last meeting, I had never imagined that Sam's speech could be that good.

By the time my turn came, I could feel that everyone was really listening to what I had to say. I could see them nodding their heads as I promised to try to find a way to raise more money for better school trips, gym equipment, and library books. At the end of my speech everybody started clapping. And they were really excited and nodding their heads and talking.

When the rally was over, we all started jumping up and down and hugging each other. Thanks to Katie, Al, Randy, and Winslow, our campaign had started with a bang.

"Three cheers for the winning team," Sam shouted, raising his arms in the air.

"We're number one!" we all shouted together. And at that moment I really felt like we had won.

Chapter Eight

When I finally left school, I was amazed at the number of kids still hanging out on the school steps. Our campaign seemed to be all that people were talking about.

We all decided to go to Fitzie's and have a celebration and plan our next strategy. The rally had been thrilling and I was feeling pretty good. But as we started talking in Fitzie's I suddenly felt as if I had a whole new set of worries. I had no idea how we could possibly top the rally.

To make matters worse, Sam was already starting to get a little too cocky. He spent the entire time at Fitzie's signing autographs. I mean, we hadn't even been elected yet and he was starting to act as stuck-up as Stacy Hansen.

By the time we left Fitzie's, I was feeling kind of discouraged. But then I remembered the poster-making meeting we were having the next day at my house. Everyone on the campaign committee would be there. If I could get them all to agree to lean on Sam to be more serious, maybe he would listen.

That night, Randy called. "Hey, Sabs," she said when I answered. "Katie, Al, and I were talking. We were thinking maybe we should expand our team for the think tank and poster-making meeting tomorrow."

"Think tank" was what Randy called the brainstorming part of the meeting, when we would decide what slogans to use on the posters.

"Definitely," I agreed. "We can use as much help as we can get." Then I told her how worried I was about Sam's attitude.

I could practically see Randy nodding as she said, "Yeah, we noticed he was acting like he'd been crowned king or something."

I wrapped one of my curls around my finger and wondered out loud, "So, who should we ask to help?"

"Katie, Al, and I already thought of that," Randy replied immediately. "I thought about how much Winslow had helped us out this afternoon. So I thought I'd call him and see if he wanted to help us out again. Then Katie suggested Nick and Jason. Katie figured that since they're Sam's best friends, they'll have the best chance of keeping him in his place."

That made me feel a lot better. As soon as I hung up I got Sam to call Nick and Jason. They both agreed to help out, and said they'd meet us all here tomorrow at two o'clock. That was the time the rest of us had agreed on.

On Saturday mornings Sam, Luke, Mark, and I all have to help out around the house. We rotate chores, and this Saturday was my day to straighten up and vacuum the downstairs. It kept me pretty busy all morning.

I was finishing up just as my dad and Mark left to do the weekly grocery shopping. That reminded me that I needed to scout out some snacks for the meeting. Running to the kitchen, I pulled open the refrigerator door.

Then I groaned. How could I have forgotten? With six people in the house, our refrigerator is always empty by the weekend. Right now the only things in it were a loaf of white bread, some butter, and half a head of lettuce. There wasn't much in the cupboards, either.

I looked at the kitchen clock. One-fifteen!

Everyone would be here in forty-five minutes. There was no way my dad and Mark would be back by then. I would have to make do with what we had.

Taking the loaf of bread from the refrigerator, I laid out ten slices. I didn't have much choice as to what to put on them. I had never heard of lettuce sandwiches before, but at least they would be low in calories. I grabbed the lettuce and washed it. Then I laid a green leaf on one of the pieces of bread, placing a second slice on top. After trimming off the crust, I cut the sandwich into four even triangles.

It looked okay, but when I bit into one of the triangles, it tasted totally bland. So I decided to add mustard on some and catsup on others. The sandwiches tasted kind of weird, but at least they were interesting. By the time I was finished, I had a whole plate of them. I arranged them neatly on the plate and placed it on the kitchen table.

Katie, Al, and Randy arrived together just as I was adding some parsley I'd found, for a garnish. Their arms were loaded down with large sheets of poster board, paints, and magic markers.

"Where should we put all this stuff?" Katie asked as the three of them burst into the house.

"In the garage," I replied, opening the door for them. Just as I started to help them carry everything out, the doorbell rang again. It was Winslow. When Winslow and I came into the kitchen, Katie, Al, and Randy had already put the supplies in the garage. But we decided to wait for the other guys before starting the posters.

My friends all looked ready to get to work. Katie was wearing dark gray sweats with a matching headband. Randy was dressed in her favorite NYU sweatshirt and ripped jeans. And Allison had on a pair of overalls and a red turtleneck, with her braid pinned into a loop at the back of her head.

I glanced down at my own outfit, jeans and this really comfortable yellow knit shirt I have. I had intended to change into something serious and presidential, but I guessed it was a good thing I hadn't had time to. I mean, presidential clothes would probably look pretty silly once I got glue or glitter or something on them.

We were just sitting down at the kitchen table when Sam walked in with Jason and

Nick. Sam, of course, made a beeline for the tray of snacks.

"This is a pretty sad looking sandwich," he pointed out, picking up a triangle and surveying it from all sides. "Looks like you forgot the meat, Sabs."

Jason and Nick started cracking up, and I could feel myself getting a little annoyed. Sam's friends were doing exactly the opposite of what I had hoped. Instead of getting him to be more serious, they were egging him on!

"Is this another 'Sabs Surprise'?" Randy asked.

Sam kept crinkling his nose and sniffing at the sandwich, until even my best friends started laughing.

I looked at my twin's red-freckled face peeking out from under his huge Uncle Sam hat. Suddenly, I felt the anger that was building up inside of me turning into laughter.

I tried to fight the laughter, but I couldn't. The whole thing was too ridiculous. Here I was getting mad at Sam over some stupid sandwiches. It wasn't my fault we didn't have anything else to put on them. *I do come up with some interesting things, though,* I thought to myself. I burst out laughing, and everyone else let loose, too. We were all hysterical, holding our sides and cracking up.

We finally managed to calm down enough to go out to the garage and start our posters. I set up my cassette player and turned on my "Rocky" motivational theme song. That put us all into high gear. We spread out the paints and paper and got to work.

"Okay, let's get this think tank going," Randy said as we unrolled a huge piece of poster board. We all put our heads together and came up with some great slogans.

Nick came up with "All's Well That Ends Wells . . . Vote Wells for Class President!"

"Sabs and Sam — Because Two Heads Are Better Than One" was Randy's contribution.

But my favorite one came from Jason. It was really plain and simple. Just . . ."Wells! Wells! Wells! FOR HEAD OF THE CLASS."

Then we got together and made the posters. It was really hard work because we needed a lot of them and we needed them to be really neat. At one point, I could tell that everyone was getting tired and a little grouchy. I realized that this was a perfect time for a surprise I had been saving. I went over to the tape deck and popped the tape out. Then I put another one in and flipped the tape player on. Suddenly the garage filled with sounds of Randy's band, Iron Wombat.

"Where did you get that tape?" asked Randy, her eyes lighting up.

"I took the liberty of making a tape during the battle of the bands," I said with a big grin.

A few weeks ago Randy had been in this super cool contest to name the best local band and Randy's band had won. For the rest of the poster-making session everyone was bopping along to the sounds of Iron Wombat.

We had such a good time that we finished sooner than I thought, and by five-thirty, everyone had left. Sam still had to take care of the leaves in our front yard, so I got stuck with the cleanup. Before I started, though, I looked at our posters, which Katie had neatly lined up on the floor to dry. There were ten of them, and they looked great.

I was screwing the covers on the paint jars when my dad and Mark turned into the driveway in my dad's new car. Dad's only had the car for two months, and it is his pride and joy.

He won't even let my mom drive it. I had already made room for the car on the other side of the garage, and my dad pulled into the space.

"Working hard, Madam President?" he asked as he kissed me on the cheek.

"We sure are," I replied, waving excitedly at the line of posters.

My dad stood back and surveyed them. "They look pretty good," he commented, nodding his head in approval. "They've got that old Sabrina sparkle." Then he and Mark started unloading groceries from the trunk. "Don't be late for dinner," Dad reminded me as he scooped up the last two bags and walked into the house.

But I wasn't really listening. "That old Sabrina sparkle," I repeated aloud. I rolled the phrase around in my head. It would make another great slogan . . . "Sabrina Sparkles"!

I started writing it in big bubble letters on a huge sheet of hot pink poster board. Then I got a great idea. I'd color the whole thing in with glitter! Then it would really sparkle!

I poured out a puddle of glue onto the lid of an old paint can. I started spreading the glue with a paintbrush, but the letters were so big, it felt like it would take forever. So I started using my fingers. My mom is always yelling at me for being messy. But when I get creative, I can't control myself.

Once the glue was in place, I reached for my jar of glitter. I needed to apply it before the glue dried. I could feel the skin on my hands starting to tighten up, so I wiped them on my jeans. Hurriedly, I poured the jar of glitter onto the letters, thanking my lucky stars that the glue was still sticky.

Then I had to figure out where to dump the excess glitter. Leaning against my dad's car, I tapped a sneaker on the floor and thought. I would empty the glitter out onto a newspaper, I decided, and then pour it back in the jar.

Satisfied, I leaned forward, but something held me back. My jeans were stuck! They were glued to my dad's new car! Trying not to panic, I pulled loose, then carefully examined the car. I breathed a sigh of relief. A little soap and water would take care of that.

I was just about to get some when Sam returned to the garage with the electric leaf blower. The blower is kind of like a giant vacuum cleaner for the garden, except it blows air out instead of sucking it in. That way you can blow the leaves into a pile instead of raking them. It was plugged into the garage outlet with a big yellow extension cord.

"Finished," Sam announced. "Boy, am I tired."

"Me too," I told him. "Could you just help me clean up the rest of this mess?"

"Just let me unplug the leaf blower. Hey, that sign looks really neat," he said, nodding to the sparkly one I'd just finished.

I'm not sure how it happened. But in the next instant Sam was tripping over the can of paint on his way to the outlet. The lid popped open, and suddenly there was paint and glue all over the floor!

As Sam pivoted around to catch his balance, he set off the leaf blower switch. The blower buzzed on with an unbelievably loud sound, sending a rainbow of glue, paint and glitter all over the garage.

To make matters worse, our dog, Cinnamon, chose that moment to come in from the backyard. He started running in circles and barking his head off. The noise of the blower must have scared him, and he was tracking glue and glitter all over the garage!

I just stood there in shock, totally unable to move. Colors and glitter were swirling all around me. I felt like I was in the middle of a tornado!

"Turn it off!" Sam shouted over the roar of the leaf blower.

Snapping out of it, I bent down and turned off the blower. Sam and I looked around the garage in disbelief. There were sparkles and paint all over the place. But the worse part was the new design pasted on my dad's new car. It looked like something from a circus.

Sam looked at me and I looked at him. We were both in shock. It seemed like the only sound left in the whole world was the sound of Cinnamon, barking.

Chapter Nine

Sam and I spent all evening Saturday and part of Sunday cleaning the garage — and Dad's car. Mark and Luke even pitched in to help; they felt so sorry for us.

We had Cinnamon to worry about, too. She's half German shepherd and half golden retriever, so we had a hard time trying to brush the glitter out of her hair. Actually, we never did manage to get all of it out. Now we always know where she's been, because after she leaves a spot, there's a pile of glitter left on the floor.

Luckily, the posters survived pretty well. Sam and I only had to do two of them over. Still, by the time Monday rolled around, we were ready to get the things out of the house!

Allison's father had agreed to take our posters to Bradley on Monday morning before school. Sam and I were waiting for him when he and Al arrived at our house early to pick us, and the posters, up. Katie, Randy, Nick, and Jason met us just inside the school's entrance.

When we got to the seventh-grade lockers, I saw that Stacy had already hung up her posters. She and Eva were standing by the lockers, giving out campaign buttons to all the kids. The buttons were laminated with a picture of Stacy standing in front of the school. Printed in a circle around the picture were the words HANSEN AND BRADLEY . . . A FAMILY TRADITION.

Some family tradition, I thought. Stacy and Eva weren't at all related, even if Stacy was the principal's daughter. The slogan was probably just to compete with the fact that Sam and I are brother and sister. I thought it was kind of unfair, but I had to admit that the buttons looked good.

I glanced around the hallway. There were Stacy for President posters plastered all over the place. They were even slicker than the buttons. Each one had a picture of Stacy and Eva shaking hands and smiling, with the words GO WITH THE WINNERS written below. And they were wearing matching red, white, and blue outfits!

I started fuming. Stacy and Eva had totally ripped off our idea! What nerve!

"It looks like everything was done by a professional photographer," Randy said as we propped our posters up against the wall.

"Sure. You can tell that the pictures were touched up," Allison added.

Allison has had some experience with modeling, so she knows all about that stuff. As I studied the poster above my head I knew that Randy had to be right. Only a professional photographer could have made "Jaws" Malone look like a human!

Looking around some more, I saw that just about the whole seventh grade was wearing Stacy buttons. And Sam and I still hadn't come up with anything to give out. I knew that the election was about a lot more than handing out freebies. But I was beginning to wonder if we would be able to convince everyone else of that.

Suddenly our posters looked very homemade next to hers. I could feel that familiar lump in my throat. Winslow Barton chose exactly that moment to come up to me. Before I knew what I was saying, I snapped, "You must have known what they were up to. Why didn't you tell me?"

"And a very good morning to you, too," Winslow replied. Then pointing to the "Sabrina Sparkles" poster that was leaning against the wall, he commented, "Nice poster."

I felt totally embarrassed, especially since Winslow didn't even seem mad that I'd yelled at him. It was ridiculous to expect him to actually spy on Stacy and Eva for me, even though I knew he supported us. I could feel my body blush starting.

"I'm sorry, Winslow," I said. "I guess I'm just nervous."

"Cheer up, Sabs," Katie said, patting my shoulder. "I think the posters look really good, too."

"Besides, good ideas are going to win the election, not posters," Allison added. "And you and Sam already proved you have tons of good ideas for Bradley."

Randy grinned at me, saying, "I can't wait until the debate on Wednesday. You and Sam are going to knock their socks off!"

My spirits felt completely restored as I

looked at my friends. They were right! So what if Stacy's posters looked professional? Ours actually said something. And it was a team project that a bunch of us had worked hard on, not just something we paid somebody to do to make us look good. Didn't that prove we would work with the whole class to make seventh grade great?

Suddenly an obnoxious voice broke into my thoughts. "Just remember, Sabrina. All is fair in love and war and school elections."

Startled, I looked up and turned around. Stacy, Eva, B.Z., and Laurel were standing right behind me.

"Better luck next year," Eva added, smiling smugly. "It's all over now."

"It's not over until it's over," Randy cut in, coming to my defense.

"Oh, sure. What are you going to do? Make cardboard campaign buttons for everyone?" Stacy scoffed. "See you at the big debate," she went on. "Good luck. You really need it now." Then they all laughed and walked away.

Boy that made me mad! But I couldn't help feeling nervous again. People were definitely wearing her buttons, and they did look cool. It just wasn't fair.

"It's just not fair," Sam said, reading my thoughts. Sometimes it's almost like we share the same mind. Twins are like that, I guess.

Sam shoved his hands deep into his pockets and kicked the floor with his sneaker. "It's not our fault that we're not rich. It's not our fault that our dad owns a hardware store instead of being the school principal!" he complained.

"Yeah. What are you supposed to do? Give out wrenches and flashlights?" Nick agreed.

"Why not?" Winslow suggested.

Katie looked at Winslow like he was a creature from outer space. "Huh?"

"Winslow, you are truly a genius," Randy said excitedly, clapping her arm around Winslow's shoulder. "We just have to use our imaginations."

Suddenly I understood what Winslow and Randy meant. "Randy's right!" I exclaimed, perking up. My mind was going a mile a minute. "We've got tons of stuff to work with." All of a sudden, I started to feel a lot better.

Just at that moment the warning bell rang.

"I'll call my dad at the store during lunch," I said in a rush. "Hey, Nick, do you think you could get Jason to come to another meeting at our house after school?"

"I guess so," he said, shrugging.

I grinned at everyone on my campaign committee. "We're not down yet!" I crowed, gathering my books. "Meeting at our house, three-thirty sharp. Winslow, you too," I added.

"Yes, sir, Madam President," he said, clicking his heels and saluting me.

Twenty-four hours later, we were all standing in the same spot by the seventh-grade lockers. But this time the story was totally different. Now there was a crowd gathered around us. I stood in the middle, proudly shaking hands and smiling at every student who passed. We had everyone's attention, and it felt great!

"Stick with Sabs and Sam," Allison called, giving out rolls of masking tape to a bunch of students.

"Don't be a drip! Vote for Sabrina!" Katie said laughing as she handed out bracelets made out of plumbing washers.

Sam was giving out mini-flashlights with slogans taped on that read, "Don't Be Left in the Dark — Vote Wells."

My dad had donated everything he could from the store. Then we had really used our imaginations to come up with a bunch of funny hardware gimmicks for our campaign.

We had tape measures with little tags that said, "Sabs and Sam Really Measure Up"; mini hand brooms with the slogan "Sabs and Sam Whisk Away the Competition" printed on them; wooden spoons that said, "Sabs and Sam Will Keep Bradley Cookin'."

My favorite gimmick was the necklaces we made out of steel hardware nuts that Randy was giving out. "You're nuts if you don't vote for Sabrina and Sam!" she kept saying.

Actually, what she had really wanted to say was: "You're nuts if you vote for Stacy Hansen!" But we all thought that was taking it a little too far. In any case, we were a hit.

Not only was everything original, but the other kids loved getting stuff they could really use. By the time lunch rolled around, there was hardly a Stacy button in sight.

"Wow! We did it again." I said beaming as Randy, Allison, Katie, and I headed for the cafeteria. I practically floated through the lunch line, picking out pineapple yogurt and an orange-flavored seltzer.

"This calls for a celebration," Katie said once we'd found a table and sat down.

"A toast to Bradley's next class president, Sabrina Wells!" Randy announced. She held up a large dill pickle that she'd pulled out of Katie's lunch bag.

Katie grabbed her tuna sandwich and held it up next to the pickle. "Here! Here!" she chimed in.

"Double that!" Allison said with a giggle, raising a stalk of celery.

With that, I held up my carton of yogurt and we all "clinked" lunches.

"You guys are the most brilliant staff in the world," I gushed. "I couldn't have done it without you."

"That's for sure," Randy joked, taking a bite of Katie's pickle.

"I think you've got the election in the bag," Allison commented.

"No doubt about it," Randy went on. "All we have to do is get you and Sam through the big debate tomorrow, get the voters to the booths, and we're all gonna have friends in high places," she said, winking at me. "There's no way Stacy's gonna win now."

I hoped she was right. But then why was that huge nervous bubble back in the pit of my stomach?

Chapter Ten

Sabrina calls Katie.

MRS.
CAMPBELL: Hello! Campbell residence.

SABRINA: Hi, Mrs. Campbell. It's Sabrina. Is Ka —

MRS.
CAMPBELL: Well, hello, Sabrina. How are you? Busy as a bee, I'll bet! I hear from Katie that you're doing a wonderful job with your campaign. You should be proud of yourself.

SABRINA: Ye-Yeah. Thank you, Mrs. Campbell. Is . . . uh . . . is Katie there? I've got to talk to her right away.

MRS.
CAMPBELL: Hold on. I'll get her for you.

KATIE: Hi, Sabs. I knew it was you the

minute I heard the phone ring.

SABRINA: I've just been dying to talk to you since lunch.

KATIE: I've been dying to talk to you, too!

SABRINA: About what? You've really got me worried. And I'm worried enough as it is.

KATIE: You are?

SABRINA: Sure. And I think it's about the same thing you're worried about.

KATIE: You mean about Stacy's disappearing act?

SABRINA: So, you noticed it, too?

KATIE: It was hard not to. The minute she saw how good the hardware gimmicks were going, she just steered clear of us. I didn't even see her or any of her gang at lunch.

SABRINA: Not a peep out of her the rest of the day. It's driving me nuts.

KATIE: Me too. Remember what happened the last time she acted this way?!

SABRINA: Yeah. That was the big campaign-button surprise. I'm really nervous about what she might pull at the debate tomorrow.

KATIE: Well, maybe Winslow can tell us something. Has he been checking up on her?

SABRINA: I'm not sure. I don't really want to ask him to spy.

KATIE: I guess you're right, but maybe you should call him.

SABRINA: I don't know. Anyway, he said he was interviewing Stacy this afternoon. He's probably with her right now.

KATIE: Then call Randy. Maybe she'll know.

SABRINA: That's a good idea.

KATIE: Call me back.

SABRINA: Okay. Bye.

Sabrina calls Randy.

MRS. ZAK: Hello.

SABRINA: Hello . . . um . . . Olivia. This is Sabrina. Is Randy there?

MRS. ZAK: Well, if it isn't the next president. Randy's kept me abreast of all the happenings, Sabrina.

SABRINA: That's great, but . . . I . . . um . . .

	I've got to talk to Randy right away. It's kind of an emergency.
MRS. ZAK:	Well, Randy's not here right now. I think she just went to Allison's house. Or, was it Katie's? I can't remember.
SABRINA:	Thanks. I'll try to reach her myself.
MRS. ZAK:	Good luck tomorrow.
SABRINA:	Thanks.

Sabrina calls Allison.

ALLISON:	Allison Cloud speaking.
SABRINA:	I'm so glad it's you and not your mother.
ALLISON:	Sabrina?
SABRINA:	Yeah, it's me. Every time I call someone I get their mother instead! And they keep talking to me about the election.
ALLISON:	I guess that's what it's like to be a celebrity.
SABRINA:	Well, it's strange. Besides, I'm not sure I'm going to be a celebrity, anyway.
ALLISON:	Why? What's wrong? Everything

is going great.

SABRINA: Well, I'm just a little nervous about the debate.

ALLISON: Aren't you and Sam ready for it?

SABRINA: Remember, we're not rehearsing it so it'll come off more naturally.

ALLISON: Well, if anyone can pull it off, you and Sam can.

SABRINA: Maybe. But what I'm really worried about is what Stacy might have up her sleeve.

ALLISON: Don't worry, Sabs.

SABRINA: I can't help it. I was thinking maybe Winslow found something out. I need to speak to Randy.

ALLISON: She just left.

SABRINA: Okay. I'll let you go. Maybe I can catch up with her at home.

ALLISON: Stop worrying, Sabs. Everything's going to be fine.

SABRINA: I hope so.

ALLISON: I know so.

SABRINA: Thanks, Al. You're a good friend.

ALLISON: Any time. Bye.

SABRINA: Bye.

As soon as Sabrina hangs up, the phone rings. She picks up at the same time as her mother does on the upstairs extension.

SABRINA: Hello!
MRS. WELLS: Hello!
SABRINA: Mom?
MRS. WELLS: Sabrina?
RANDY: Hey, Mrs. Wells. Hey, Sabs.
SABRINA: Mom, it's Randy. You can hang up now.
MRS. WELLS: Hello, Randy. How are you? We haven't seen enough of you since this campaign started.
RANDY: We've all been pretty busy with the election and —
SABRINA: Mom, would you puh-leaze get off the phone. We have important stuff to talk about.
MRS. WELLS: Okay, Sabrina. I'll let you guys talk. Good luck tomorrow. I certainly hope you win!

RANDY: Thanks, Mrs. Wells. Good-bye.

MRS. WELLS: Good-bye, Randy. Don't stay on too long, Sabrina. Dinner's in fifteen minutes.

SABRINA: Okay, Mom.

MRS. WELLS: Bye.

SABRINA: BYE!!

RANDY: Is she off yet?

SABRINA: I think so. Boy, I'm having a heck of a time with mothers today. First Katie's. Then yours. Now mine. When was the last time you spoke to Winslow?

RANDY: Just now.

SABRINA: And?

RANDY: AND??? And nothing.

SABRINA: What do you mean, nothing? Has he been tracking down Stacy?

RANDY: Sure. She gave him an interview this afternoon.

SABRINA: And?

RANDY: And . . . nothing. Everything's status quo.

SABRINA: I hope you stop using these big

words after tomorrow, because I'm not sure what they mean.

RANDY: You make it sound like you don't expect to win.

SABRINA: Well . . .

RANDY: I told you. The election's in the bag.

SABRINA: I'm not so sure, Ran. I'm afraid of what Stacy might be up to. She was too quiet today. It's making me crazy.

RANDY: Exactly.

SABRINA: Exactly? Exactly what?

RANDY: She's just trying to psyche you out.

SABRINA: What?

RANDY: She's got nothing left. The election is tomorrow, you and Sam won everybody over today, and all she's got left is to try to drive you crazy . . . and it sounds like she's doing a great job!

SABRINA: You know, I never thought about it that way. I think you're right.

RANDY: I know I'm right. Candidates do it all the time. It's a strategy. A pretty slick one. But a strategy just the same.

SABRINA: So, what am I supposed to do?

RANDY: Just calm down and win the election. We've done everything we could. Now all you and Sam have to do is be yourselves and win the debate. The rest . . . as they say . . . is history.

SABRINA: Thanks, Ran. That makes me feel a lot better.

RANDY: Don't mention it. Just get a good night's rest. Tomorrow's gonna be a big day.

SABRINA: Thanks again, Randy. Oh! And, Ran.

RANDY: What?

SABRINA: Could you just do me one more favor?

RANDY: Say the word.

SABRINA: Could you call Katie for me and tell her what you just told me? I've been tying up the phone for too long.

RANDY: No problem. See you tomorrow.

SABRINA: Thanks again and again. Bye!

RANDY: Bye.

Randy calls Allison.

ALLISON: Allison Cloud speaking.

RANDY: Hey, Al. It's me.

ALLISON: Did you talk to Sabs about what we talked about?

RANDY: Yeah. I just got off the phone with her. But I heard she called you. Why didn't you tell her that we think Stacy is just trying to fake her out?

ALLISON: Well, she wanted to talk to you, and I just figured that it wouldn't look too good if she knew we were discussing it. It would make it sound like we were as worried as she is.

RANDY: That was a good idea. No reason for all four of us to be nervous wrecks.

ALLISON: So? Did she go for it?

RANDY: I think so. Anyway, she sounds a lot calmer now. I mean, it's okay for us to be worried about Stacy, but Sabs and Sam have to be in tip-top shape.

ALLISON: I agree. We should probably fill Katie in.

RANDY: Okay. I'll call her. Ciao.

ALLISON: Good-bye, Randy.

Chapter Eleven

I tossed and turned all night long. No matter what I did, I couldn't seem to fall asleep for more than a few minutes. The night seemed to last a million years.

First I tried listening to the radio, but that didn't help. Then I tried counting sheep. But they all started looking like Stacy Hansen. And that gave me a stomachache. Finally, I sat up and switched on the light beside my bed.

I was really nervous about the debate. The voting was happening right afterward, so if we didn't do well in the debate, there was no way we'd win the election.

Sam and our campaign committee had convinced me that it would be better if we didn't rehearse. Allison thought that we would show more natural enthusiasm, without seeming stiff and practiced.

But still . . . the thought of not having my

lines ready gave me goose bumps all over. I mean, even though I love being on stage, I was having nightmares about what kinds of questions might come up. Then I remembered all that Randy had said. I decided it wouldn't do any good if I fell asleep during the debate. I switched off the light and snuggled down between the covers.

Sometime during the night I had this weird dream. I was at the debate, standing on the stage in front of this big silver curtain. There were loads of exotic plants and flowers all over the place, and the whole school was waiting for me to speak. But I had my eggplant outfit on, and I couldn't think of anything to say because I was sure that my orange tights were going to fall down around my knees at any minute!

Everybody started chanting, "Speak! Speak!" But I couldn't move. I just stood there, looking out into the auditorium, when suddenly this plant in front of me came to life and started nibbling on the sleeve of my eggplant blouse. It kept growing bigger and bigger, until finally it was a giant Venus's flytrap opening it's mouth . . . ready to grab me . . . And then I woke up.

After that, I gave up on trying to sleep. I just

lay in bed and listened to my "Rocky" tape on my Walkman. By the time my alarm went off, I had already done my exercises and eaten breakfast. I was happy about that, since I wanted to take my time getting dressed.

I took an extra long shower, since everyone else was still asleep. I hardly ever get to do that with my brothers around, so it felt like a real treat. Then I went up to my room and opened my closet door.

I knew that Stacy was going to have one of her new incredible outfits. I started flipping through clothes. Nothing in my closet came close to Stacy's glamorous wardrobe. Finally, I gave up. I wanted people to vote for me because of my ideas, not because I had better clothes than Stacy. I decided that my best clothes strategy was to just look like me. Suddenly, I felt one hundred percent better. I looked through my closet again and decided to wear my blue skirt with the triangles all over it and the matching vest with a gold turtleneck. I decided to wear my hair loose because that was most like me.

I did want to give myself one special treat, so I decided to use some cologne I got for my birthday. Trouble was, I kept the cologne on my shelf in the bathroom. After I got dressed, I ran down the attic steps to the bathroom.

"Hey, you're not president yet," Sam joked as I slipped into the bathroom just ahead of him to grab the cologne. "Give someone else a chance!"

Before he could say another word I was back out in the hallway, the cologne in my hand. "Ready for the big day?" he asked me. He had a kind of nervous look on his face.

"As ready as I'll ever be," I answered.

"Don't sweat it, little sister," he assured me as he set up a collection of bottles and tubes on the bathroom sink. He had hair spray, styling gel, cologne, tooth polish, a razor, and shaving cream.

What he was thinking of using the shaving cream for I hadn't a clue, since Sam doesn't have anything that even slightly resembles a whisker on his face. I decided not to say anything about that, though. I read in *Young Chic* that joking comments can sometimes destroy a person's ego. And I definitely did not want to do that to Sam today!

"You're up early today," my mom commented, passing me in the hallway as Sam shut the bathroom door. She looked at me with a kind of warm glow in her eyes. "Come into my room. I want to give you a little something for good luck."

I went and sat at the foot of my mom and dad's bed while she took a small box from her top dresser drawer and handed it to me.

"What's this?" I asked, shaking the box.

"Try opening it," Mom suggested with a smile.

My first thought was that it was a rabbit's foot or something. But when I opened the box, I saw that it was something a zillion times better.

"A Bradley pin! It's perfect!" I cried, jumping up to give her a hug. It was a gold rectangle with a raised *B* in the center of it, surrounded by the school's logo.

My mom's eyes actually got a little misty as she explained, "That's the pin your father gave me when he first asked me to go steady with him. I thought maybe it would bring you and Sam good luck."

"Mom . . ." For a second I was speechless. That was a first! Then I gave her another hug. "You're the best!"

I was beaming as I pinned it on my blazer. Whenever I looked at it, I would remember how special the pin was to my mom and how proud she was of Sam and me. It was just the extra support I needed. I was determined not to let her, or myself, down.

By the time I got to school, Katie was already at our locker, and Randy and Allison were with her.

"Sabrina, you look great!" Katie exclaimed, giving me the once-over.

"Cool pin, Sabs!" Randy commented. She pointed to the lapel of my blazer. "Is it an antique?" Randy's really into antique clothing and stuff. Acorn Falls has only one thrift store, but Randy is a devoted regular there.

"Sort of," I replied, giggling. Boy, would my mom kill me if she heard that! "It was my mom's school pin."

"It's really nice," Allison said as she peered at it.

"The seventh-grade math room is packed," Katie informed me.

I felt my stomach flutter like it had a million butterflies in it. The thing that worried me the most about the debate was that it was being held in the math room. I hoped that wasn't a bad omen. It seemed that nothing ever went right for me in that room. At least the debate was happening during first period and my math class was canceled. I decided that *that* was a good omen. In an hour, the whole thing would be over.

I took a deep breath. "We'd better get going. Sam said he'd meet us there."

Sam was waiting outside the math classroom. He was wearing his navy blazer with a white shirt, and he had his hair slicked back. He looked really sharp.

"Five minutes, candidates," Mr. Gray called out. Mr. Gray is our social studies teacher, and he's really gorgeous. I had a giant crush on him at the beginning of the year. I was sure glad he was running the debate, instead of Miss Munson.

"Remember," Katie said as she smoothed out the lapel of my blazer, "we'll be in sitting in the front, right in the middle."

"So if you get stuck, just look down," Allison added.

"Yeah. We'll coach you," Randy assured me.

Then they all wished Sam and me good luck

and headed for their seats. It was hard to say good-bye. I would have felt a million times better if they were coming onto the stage with me.

The next thing I knew, Mr. Gray was clapping his hands and calling, "Places, candidates. We're starting."

We all lined up in front of Miss Munson's desk. We were all standing in a row. Eva, Stacy, me, and Sam. Stacy was wearing this knockout new purple knit dress. Of course, she had matching pumps.

Standing there, I was suddenly reminded of the dream I'd had. I was glad to see that there wasn't any silver curtain, just the blinds at the windows. But I checked for any unusual-looking plants, just in case. Luckily there were none.

Just as Mr. Gray started quieting down the audience, Sam stuck his hand into his breast pocket and pulled out a pair of sunglasses.

"What are you doing?" I whispered under my breath.

"Chill, Sabs. They'll love it," he whispered back. "The shades make me look cool."

"You're supposed to look like the vice president," I said, clenching my teeth together. "Not

Bruce Willis."

"Don't sweat it," he replied, adjusting his shades.

"Hope you're not a sore loser," Stacy muttered under her breath as she flashed a big smile for the audience.

I ignored her, remembering what my best friends had told me about Stacy just trying to psyche me out.

"And now, I'd like to introduce the candidates," Mr. Gray began.

My mind went blank. As Stacy smiled and waved, everything seemed to be happening in a fuzzy dream.

" . . . and running for vice president of the seventh grade, Sam Wells . . ." Mr. Gray went on.

I watched as Sam shifted his shoulders and made a deep bow. And then Mr. Gray was announcing my name.

" . . . our second candidate for seventh-grade president, Sabrina Wells."

The sound of clapping brought me out of my fog. Blinking, I waved at everyone and tried to smile.

Then the questioning started. Stacy and Eva

went first. From the stiff way they answered Mr. Gray's questions, you could tell that they had a speech prepared. But I couldn't help feeling nervous when Mr. Gray turned to Sam and me.

"Sabrina," Mr. Gray began, "during your campaign, you mentioned that you think seventh graders should be given first aid training."

"Yes, sir," I answered, happy to have an easy question. "I believe that we shouldn't have to wait until the eighth grade to have CPR training. There's no reason to wait that long to learn how to save lives."

That got a round of applause. I was happy with my answer.

Sam waited for the clapping to die down, then added, ". . . and I think the best way to save lives at Bradley is to close down the cafeteria immediately!"

The whole auditorium burst out laughing. I was mortified. This was supposed to be a serious debate, and there was Sam throwing out one-liners! He was going to make us lose the election.

When Mr. Gray asked Sam his next question, about teamwork, I automatically started to cringe. What was Sam going to say now? That everyone at Bradley should team up and join the circus?

I was glad to see that at least Sam took off those dumb sunglasses. Then, giving me a quick smile, he said, "Sabrina and I are serious about teaming up for Bradley Junior High . . ."

Was I hearing correctly, or was Sam Wells, campaign clown, actually being sincere?

". . . we feel a serious commitment to include serious activities and clubs for each and every one of our classmates . . . ."

He went on to talk about the teamwork that had gone into our poster-making sessions and how we would try to bring that same spirit to the whole class. His answer would have been perfect, except for one thing.

He kept on using the word *serious* over and over again, until his answer didn't sound serious at all!

". . . But seriously, Sabrina and I are serious about working seriously together with all our classmates to make the coming year the most serious year ever!"

When he stopped talking, Sam just grinned at me. The applause was thunderous.

I couldn't believe it. He was a hit! Despite his being stuck on the word *serious*, I was really proud of Sam's answer. And I knew he had done it for me. I grinned at Sam, wanting him to know how much that meant to me.

The rest of the debate passed in a blur. Finally, it was over.

Before I could even move, Stacy cornered me.

"You and your stupid brother really did it this time," she fumed. Then she angrily stomped away.

"Creeps!" Eva sputtered. "You guys don't play fair!"

What were they talking about? I wondered as I watched her run off after Stacy.

Suddenly, Sam and I were surrounded by a crowd of kids. I saw Katie, Al, and Randy trying to cut through.

Randy shook her fist above the crowd. "We did it!" she shouted.

"You guys were great!" Katie shrieked.

Allison didn't say anything, but just gave me a great big hug.

"I told you, you and Sam make a great team," Randy said, clapping both of us on the shoulder. "Come on! Let's go cast our votes."

The "voting booth" was a curtained-off area at the back of the math classroom. I waited in the line of seventh graders until it was my turn. It felt weird to see my name on the ballot. And even weirder to vote for myself. But I did it.

Then I waited for Sam and my friends. The results wouldn't be in until lunchtime, two whole class periods away. Everyone was acting so sure that Sam and I had won. But I tried not to think about it. I wouldn't even talk about it. I didn't want to jinx anything.

Band and English classes went by in a blur. I don't know how I made it to the cafeteria at lunchtime, but suddenly I found myself at a table with a tray of lasagna in front of me. Sam, Katie, Al, Randy, Winslow, Nick, and Jason were there, too. Everyone kind of picked at their food halfheartedly. I know I couldn't eat a single bite of mine.

Finally I heard the first crackle of the loudspeaker. Everyone at our table held hands.

"The results are in," Mr. Hansen's crackly voice was the only sound in the cafeteria.

"It must be killing him to announce that his precious daughter lost," Randy whispered.

"Shhssh," I cautioned her. "We haven't won yet."

I could feel Stacy and her clones watching us, but I couldn't look in their direction. My heart was beating so fast, I felt like it would jump right out of my chest.

The eighth-grade winners were announced first. I couldn't stand the suspense. I thought I was going to die!

". . . and now for the seventh grade . . ." Mr. Hansen went on. I felt Sam cross his fingers. Then, all the way down the table, we all crossed our fingers. I held my breath.

"Congratulations to Sab . . ."

I screamed so loud, I couldn't even hear the rest. We all jumped up and raised our arms in the air at the same time. "Yay!" we all shouted.

"We did it! We did it!" we all screamed. Then, before I knew it, someone was lifting me and Sam up in the air. Even though I didn't have my Walkman on, I could hear "Rocky," my motivational theme song, playing loud and clear in my head.

"Sam, you're the greatest!" I shouted above the crowd.

"That goes double for you, twin sister!" he

shouted back.

Looking down, I saw Stacy, Eva, B.Z., and Laurel storming out of the cafeteria.

The rest of the afternoon was amazing. Everywhere I went people came up and congratulated me. Even people I didn't know. Even teachers!

By the end of the day I was exhausted. I was leaning against my locker after the final bell when I suddenly heard, "Sabrina! Sam! Let's go to Fitzie's and celebrate!" That made me think of Stacy and the ice-cream cones.

And then I remembered, no matter what stuff Stacy gave to the kids, nothing had been as great as what my best friends or my twin brother had given me.

I wouldn't trade them in for all the ice cream in the world!

Look for these titles in the GIRL TALK series

1 WELCOME TO JUNIOR HIGH!
Introducing the Girl Talk characters, Sabrina Wells, Katie Campbell, Randy Zak, and Allison Cloud. When our four heroines meet and have to plan the first junior high dance of the year, the results are hilarious.

2 FACE-OFF!
Katie Campbell is just plain fed up with being "perfect." But when she decides to join the boys' ice hockey team, she gets more than she bargained for.

3 THE NEW YOU
Allison Cloud's world turns upside down when she is chosen to model for *Belle* magazine with Stacy the Great!

4 REBEL, REBEL
Randy Zak is acting even stranger than usual. Could a visit from her cute New York friend have something to do with it?

5 IT'S ALL IN THE STARS
Sabrina gets even when she discovers that someone is playing a practical joke on her — and all her horoscopes are coming true.

6 THE GHOST OF EAGLE MOUNTAIN
The girls go on a weekend ski trip, only to discover that they're sleeping on the very spot where the Ghost of Eagle Mountain wanders!

7 **ODD COUPLE**

When a school project pairs goody-two-shoes, Mark Wright, with super-hip Randy Zak as "parents" of an egg, Randy and Mark find out that they actually have something in common.

8 **STEALING THE SHOW**

Sabrina sets out to prove that she's perfect for the lead role in the school production of *Grease*, only to land herself in one crazy mix-up after another.

9 **PEER PRESSURE**

Katie Campbell doesn't know whether to laugh or cry when Stacy the Great's best friend Laurel Spencer is chosen as her skating partner for the Winter Carnival.

10 **FALLING IN LIKE**

Allison's not happy about having to tutor seventh-grade troublemaker Billy Dixon. But when they discover a key to his problems, Allison finds out that you can't always judge a book by its cover.

11 **MIXED FEELINGS**

A gorgeous Canadian boy moves to Acorn Falls and joins the hockey team. Suddenly life turns pretty interesting for Katie Campbell — especially when she finds out that Sabrina likes the new boy.

12 **DRUMMER GIRL**

It's time for the annual 'Battle of the Bands'. Randy decides to start her own all-girl band after she overhears the guys in Acorn Falls say that girls can't play rock 'n' roll!

13 **THE WINNING TEAM**
It's a fight to the finish when Sabrina and Sam run against Stacy the great and Eva Malone for president and vice-president of the seventh grade!

14 **EARTH ALERT!**
Allison, Katie, Sabrina, and Randy try to convince Bradley junior high to turn the annual seventh grade fun fair into a fair to save the Earth!

15 **ON THE AIR**
Randy lands the after-school job of her dreams, as the host of a one-hour radio program. But she 's not so sure being a celebrity is all that great!

16 **HERE COMES THE BRIDE**
There's going to be a wedding in Acorn Falls! When Katie's mom announces plans to remarry, Katie learns that she's also getting a step-brother.

17 **STAR QUALITY**
When Sabrina's favorite game show comes to Acorn Falls, she's determined to get on the show, *and* get her friends to be part of her act.

18 **KEEPING THE BEAT**
Randy's band Iron Wombat is more popular than ever after winning the Battle of the Bands. But Randy's excitement turns sour when the band is booked for Stacy the great's birthday bash!

TALK BACK!

TELL US WHAT YOU THINK ABOUT GIRL TALK

Name ______________________________

Address ______________________________

City ____________ State _____ Zip _________

Birthday Day _____ Mo. _______ Year _____

Telephone Number (____) ______________

1) On a scale of 1 (The Pits) to 5 (The Max), how would you rate Girl Talk? Circle One:

1 2 3 4 5

2) What do you like most about Girl Talk?

___Characters___Situations___Telephone Talk

Other ______________________________

3) Who is your favorite character? Circle One:

Sabrina Katie Randy

Allison Stacy Other

4) Who is your least favorite character?

____

5) What do you want to read about in Girl Talk?

____

____

Send completed form to :

Western Publishing Company, Inc.
1220 Mound Avenue Mail Station #85
Racine, Wisconsin 53404